Charlie and the Castle

First published in 2006 by
Franklin Watts
338 Euston Road
London
NW1 3BH

Franklin Watts Australia
Hachette Children's Books
Level 17/207 Kent Street
Sydney
NSW 2000

A CIP catalogue record for this book is available from the British Library.

ISBN (10) 0 7496 6601 3 (hbk)
ISBN (13) 978-0-7496-6601-9 (hbk)
ISBN (10) 0 7496 6896 2 (pbk)
ISBN (13) 978-0-7496-6896-9 (pbk)

Series Editor: Jackie Hamley
Series Advisor: Dr Hilary Minns
Series Designer: Peter Scoulding

Printed in China

Charlie and the Castle

by Sue Graves

Illustrated by Gwyneth Williamson

W
FRANKLIN WATTS
LONDON • SYDNEY

Sue Graves

"Do you like bouncy castles? You never know, but the next time you go in one, you might meet the king and his knights, too!"

Gwyneth Williamson

"I think that having a bouncy castle all to myself would be brilliant!"

The Fun Day was over.

Bert was packing up.

Teddies

"Can I have one more go?" asked Charlie.

"Yes," said Bert.
"But you'll be lonely
in there on your own."

Charlie bounced

and bounced.

The king of the castle came.
He bounced, too.

The knights of the castle came. They bounced, too.

They all had lots of fun.

“Time to go!” called Bert.

“Were you lonely, Charlie?” asked Bert.

"No," said Charlie.
"I wasn't lonely at all!"

Notes for adults

TADPOLES is structured to provide support for newly independent readers. The stories may also be used by adults for sharing with young children.

Starting to read alone can be daunting. **TADPOLES** helps by providing visual support and repeating words and phrases. These books will both develop confidence and encourage reading and rereading for pleasure.

If you are reading this book with a child, here are a few suggestions:

1. Make reading fun! Choose a time to read when you and the child are relaxed and have time to share the story.

2. Talk about the story before you start reading. Look at the cover and the blurb. What might the story be about? Why might the child like it?

3. Encourage the child to reread the story, and to retell the story in their own words, using the illustrations to remind them what has happened.

4. Discuss the story and see if the child can relate it to their own experience, or perhaps compare it to another story they know.

5. Give praise! Remember that small mistakes need not always be corrected.

If you enjoyed this book, why not try another TADPOLES story?